HERE AND THERE

The Puerto Ricans

Tana Reiff

A Pacemaker® **HOPES** *and* **DREAMS 2** Book

FEARON/JANUS/QUERCUS
Belmont, California

Simon & Schuster Supplementary Education Group

HOPES *and* DREAMS 2

FAIR FIELDS *The Filipinos*
HERE AND THERE *The Puerto Ricans*
MAKING HEAVEN *The Koreans*
MANY MILES *The Arabs*
NEVER SO GOOD *The Jamaicans*
SENT AWAY *The Japanese*
THE NEXT LIFE *The Indians*
TIES TO THE PAST *The Poles*
TWO HEARTS *The Greeks*
WHO IS MY NEIGHBOR? *The Salvadorans*

Cover photo: Alex Quesada/Matrix International, Inc.
Cover Design: Rucker Huggins
Illustration: Duane Bibby

ISBN 0–8224–3807–0
Library of Congress Catalog Card Number: 92–71062

Printed in the United States of America
   9 8 7 6 5
MA

CONTENTS

1 A Working Wife 1

2 Missing the Children 8

3 The Children Come Up 13

4 Trouble in Puerto Rico 20

5 Life in *El Barrio* 27

6 Very Bad News 33

7 Together Is What Matters ... 41

8 To the South Bronx 47

9 Keeping Out of Trouble 54

10 Fighting Fires 59

11 New Plans 64

12 A Home in Camden 70

1 A Working Wife

New York City, 1965

Gloria Colón Martinez
felt very alone.
Her children were far away,
and her husband Hector
was at work.
He had gotten up
very early in the morning.
His job in a radio factory
was across the river,
in New Jersey.
It took him over an hour
to get there.
He had to take
the subway and two buses.

Gloria sat by herself
at the kitchen table.
It was almost noon,
but the lights were on.
It was always dark

in the tiny apartment
unless the lights
were turned on.
There was only one window,
and it opened
onto an air shaft.

Gloria and Hector had to climb
four flights of stairs
to get to the apartment.
But they were glad
they had a place to live
in Spanish Harlem.
They had come from Puerto Rico
less than three weeks ago.
Now they had an apartment,
and Hector had found a job.

As Gloria sat in her kitchen,
she listened to the many sounds
the big building was making.
She heard the water
rushing down the pipes.
She heard the heat pipes
bang and crash
as if they were just too old

to do their job.
She heard other people's children
crying and screaming
from the other apartments.
She heard the mothers
shouting in Spanish.

"This building is so noisy,"
Gloria said to herself.
"Oh, but I wish the noise
was our children.
It's very strange
to be without my babies.
I've never been away from them."

In her mind,
Gloria heard her little twins,
Inez and Susana,
crying for her.
She felt Carolina and José Miguel
hanging onto her dress.
She held the hand of José Alonzo,
the four-year-old,
as they walked down the street.
He always wanted
to hold his mother's hand.

And Gloria saw
her first child, José Luis,
sitting in her lap.
He was nine years old,
but he still liked to sit
in his mother's lap.
Gloria loved all her children,
but José Luis was her favorite.
She called him "the good one."
As Gloria sat in her kitchen
in Spanish Harlem,
her eyes filled with tears.

When Hector and Gloria
came to New York,
they had to leave their children
back in Puerto Rico.
The children were staying
with *compadres*—
good friends of the family
who were willing
to take care of them.
The three older children
were at one place,
and the three younger ones
were at another place.

Gloria remembered
how the children
had cried their eyes out
when she and Hector
said good-bye to them.
Gloria and Hector had promised
to bring the children
to New York
as soon as they
could buy them plane tickets.
Now that Hector had a job,
Gloria knew
that she would have to
find a job, too.

Later that day,
Mrs. Santiago,
the woman next door,
said she would go along with Gloria
to look for a job.
The sewing factories downtown
needed help.
Gloria knew how to use
a sewing machine.
She was pretty sure
she could get a job.

She was right.
That night when Hector came home,
she told him the news.
"I start tomorrow,"
she told him.
"You and I both have jobs!
And Mrs. Santiago next door, too.
How about that?"

"I'm not used
to a working wife,"
said Hector.
"But we have to do this
to get the children up here.
Everything is so poor
down in Puerto Rico.
Here they can go
to better schools
and make something of themselves!"

"Puerto Ricans like us
have been coming up here
for 40 years already,"
said Gloria.
"We all want the same thing."

Thinking It Over

1. Have you ever felt alone
   when there is noise
   all around you?

2. Why can it be hard
   for children and parents
   to be apart from each other?

3. Why do you think
   Hector and Gloria
   are in New York
   without their children?

4. What is "the same thing"
   that everyone wants?

2 Missing the Children

Gloria and Mrs. Santiago
took the subway to work
early every morning.
They worked hard
all day long,
making one dress after another.
Soon a whole month
had gone by.
Gloria and Mrs. Santiago
were still making dresses.
They worked faster than ever.

"We Puerto Ricans
make the clothes now,"
said Mrs. Santiago one day.
She did not look up
as she worked.
"Long ago the Irish and Germans
did these jobs.
Then the Italians and Jews.
Now it is us.

They all moved up
to better things.
So maybe we are next."

"I have high hopes,"
said Gloria.
"I keep thinking about
my six children.
We don't have enough money
to pay for Catholic school.
Puerto Rico is so crowded
that the public schools
can only give the children
a half day of school.
You can't learn enough
in only half a day.
There aren't enough jobs, either.
Our only hope is up here.
I'm going to work and work
to bring every child to New York.
Oh, but I miss them so much.
I can't stand it."

"Why don't you go down there
and bring them up yourself?"
said Mrs. Santiago.

"Put your pennies away.
Then you can go get your babies."

"Maybe I will,"
said Gloria.

She told Hector,
but he said,
"We should save our money
to buy plane tickets
for all the children.
Why waste money
on tickets for you?"

"You don't understand,"
said Gloria.
"If I don't see my babies soon,
I will go out of my mind!"

"Gloria, I miss the children
just as much as you do,"
said Hector.
"But they can come up
by themselves.
The other people on the plane
can watch out for them."

That wasn't good enough
for Gloria.
So every week when she got paid,
she put a few dollars
in a little box under the bed.
Hector had no idea
she was putting money away.

One day, many months later,
she told her boss
that she had to leave her job
for a few weeks.
Then she bought a ticket
to San Juan, Puerto Rico.

The next morning,
as soon as Hector
left for the radio factory,
she wrote him a note.
"Understand my heart,"
the note began.
"I must go and get my babies.
We will all be back soon."
Then she got a ride
to the airport
and flew to San Juan.

Thinking It Over

1. Do you believe
   that a wife must always listen
   to her husband?
   Why or why not?

2. Have you ever
   saved up for something
   that you really wanted?

3. Has someone ever
   put an idea into your head
   that you went ahead with?

3 The Children Come Up

Hector was angry
when he found Gloria's note.
But he did understand her heart.
Gloria was a mother
above all else.
To be away from her children
was like tearing her heart out.
So he waited for her
to return with the children.

A few days later
Hector got a letter
from Gloria.
She told him
when to meet her and the children
at the airport.

The next week,
Hector went to the airport
to meet his family.
He spotted Gloria

coming off the plane.
Then he saw
five children with her.
Gloria was carrying the twins,
Inez and Susana.
Carolina and José Miguel
hung onto her dress.
And José Luis,
"the good one,"
walked along behind his mother.

"Where is José Alonzo?"
Hector wanted to know.

"He stayed behind,"
said Gloria.
"He wanted to stay
with his *compadres.*
He did not want to come
here to the mainland."

Hector was not happy
that Gloria had left one child
behind in Puerto Rico.
But what could he do?

Everyone else was here now.
And with children sleeping
all over the floor
in the tiny apartment,
it would be hard to fit one more.

In the next few days,
the children began their new life
in New York City.
Gloria got the older children
started in school.
Then she went back
to the sewing factory
to ask for her job back.

"Very well,"
said the boss.
He looked at the twins
Gloria had with her.
Little Inez and Susana
looked back at the man
and gave him sweet smiles.
"What are you going to do
with these children?"
asked the boss.

"I will look for someone
to take care of them,"
said Gloria.

Back in Puerto Rico,
there was always someone
to watch your children.
But back in Puerto Rico,
Gloria did not have a job.
She never had to find someone
to watch children all day long,
every day of the week.
This was not so easy
here on the mainland.
So when Gloria
went back to work
at the sewing factory,
she brought Inez and Susana
along with her.

The sewing factory
was not a safe place
for small children to play.
There were little bits of cloth
flying around the air.
The floor was dirty.

Every now and then
a needle broke
and flew off a machine.
Sometimes Gloria had to stop
to help one of the children.

  "This is not working out,"
the boss told her one day.
"You must find child care
or leave this job.
We can't have these children here
day after day."

  That night Gloria wanted
to talk about the problem.
But first Hector
had something to say.

  "Bad news, bad news,"
he began.
"The radio factory
is going to close down.
They are opening a new factory
down in Puerto Rico.
How about that?
I come up here for work

and the work goes back there!
Anyway, I'm out of a job."

"That's very bad news,"
said Gloria.
"But maybe this will help
with another problem.
Maybe you can watch the babies
while I go to work."

"Me? Watch kids?"
Hector said.

"Well, we can't both
be out of work, can we?"
said Gloria.

And so Gloria kept her job
at the sewing factory
and Hector watched the kids.
It was hard on Hector,
and hard on everyone
trying to live on only Gloria's pay.

Thinking It Over

1. Have there ever been times
   when your family
   was not all in one place?

2. These days,
   what are some different ways
   for children to be taken care of
   while their parents go to work?

3. Why do some companies
   move their factories
   off the mainland
   or to other countries?

4 Trouble in Puerto Rico

Hector watched the kids
for a few weeks.
He didn't enjoy it at all.
He wasn't used to being
with little children all day.
Most of all,
he couldn't stand to see Gloria
going off to work every day
when he had no job himself.
Hector had always felt
it was a man's job
to take care of his family.

So one night he said,
"Gloria, I can't go on
like this.
I have to find a job."

"I know this has been
hard for you,"
said Gloria.

"I'll stay home from work
for a few days.
You go look for a job."

Hector threw his arms
around his wife.
"I'll be working again soon,"
he said.

Hector visited factories
all over New York City.
But everywhere he went,
he was told
to check back later.

The next week,
Gloria stayed home
a few more days.
Hector went out again,
but his luck was no better.

By this time
Hector was feeling very bad.
He was afraid
that he would never find
a job in New York.

One day he said,
"Gloria, I have made up my mind.
I am going back to Puerto Rico.
I'll get a job
in the radio factory down there."

"You'll find another job
here on the mainland,"
said Gloria.

"Don't be so sure,"
said Hector.
"So many factories
are leaving the country.
People work for less money
in other parts of the world.
Why should I hold out hope
for a job here?
I'll make less in Puerto Rico,
but at least it's a job."

"What am I going to do
with these children?"
Gloria asked.

"I can take them along,"
said Hector.

"No, I can't let them go again,"
said Gloria.
"In fact,
I want José Alonzo
up here, too."

"I will go to Puerto Rico,"
said Hector.
"I will find work
and send José Alonzo up."

"But how will I
take care of these children
and keep my job?"
asked Gloria.
"How will I feed them
and pay the rent, too?"

"You can go on welfare,"
said Hector.
"What else can you do?"

Gloria cried and cried.
She could see that Hector
was probably right.
There was no way
to keep the family together
in one place right now.
There was no way
she could take care of children
and work, too.

So Hector went to Puerto Rico.

As soon as he got to San Juan,
he went to the home
of José Alonzo's *compadres*.
He wanted to see the boy
and he needed a place to stay.
Then he went to the radio factory
to get a job.

When he got to the factory,
he saw a long line of people
waiting outside.
"What's going on?"
he asked the man
at the end of the line.

"We're waiting
to put our names in
for a job here,"
said the man.
"They filled all the jobs
the first week
the factory opened.
We have to sign up
and then wait
till a job opens up."

Hector's heart sank.
He knew he had made
a big mistake.
He shouldn't have counted on
getting a job
at the new radio factory.
He wished he had made plans
with the company
before he came all this way.
Now he was as out of work
at this factory
as he had been
at the one in New Jersey.

Thinking It Over

1. How would you feel
   if you were a man out of work
   when your wife has a job?

2. If you were Gloria,
   would you go on welfare now?

3. If you were Hector,
   would you have gone back
   to Puerto Rico?
   Why or why not?

5 Life in *El Barrio*

Up in New York,
Gloria had to leave her job
and go on welfare and food stamps.
She saw no other way
to take care of the children.

When the first welfare check
came in the mail,
Gloria was a bit surprised
at how small it was.
She wondered
how she would make ends meet
on so little money.
Still, it was more
than she would get in Puerto Rico.
Every month Gloria made sure
that the rent was paid.
And when she took the children
down to the corner *bodega*
to buy food,
she didn't let them

buy any candy.
Every cent mattered.

Now that Hector wasn't around,
Gloria found herself
going out more often
into Spanish Harlem—*El Barrio*.
She enjoyed going to the *bodega*
because they always had
all the Puerto Rican foods.
There were the plantains,
the large green bananas
she had always loved.
There were mangos,
such a sweet yellow fruit.
Of course, there were rice and beans,
which Gloria cooked every night.
And she often bought dried salt pork
because the fresh pork or chicken
just cost too much.

Almost every night
Gloria would sit out front
and talk with the neighbors
and listen to the boys
playing their *bongos* or *conga* drums.

Everyone sang along in Spanish,
while the children climbed
up and down the fire escapes
and ran all over the place.
Sometimes someone on the block
would ask Gloria and the children
to join their pig roast
at the playground.

"Why don't you come along
to my church?"
Mrs. Santiago asked Gloria one day.

"Oh, I'm Catholic,"
said Gloria.

"Doesn't matter,"
said Mrs. Santiago.
"Our little store-front church
is open to everyone!"

So Gloria took the children
and went along
to Mrs. Santiago's little church.
It was very different
from the Catholic church.

It was in a building
that was once a store.
Everyone welcomed Gloria
like an old friend.
The preacher was
a Puerto Rican man
who lived down the block.
The Spanish words he spoke
sounded like music to Gloria.
He really made people
wake up and think.

This church made Gloria
feel like part of something.
She had not felt that way
since she left Puerto Rico.
So she kept on going
to the little store-front church,
even if she did think of herself
as Catholic.

Then Mrs. Santiago
started taking Gloria
to the *botánica*.
This little shop
was full of candles,

special herbs,
and religious charms.
"The Catholic church
might look down
on a place like this,"
said Gloria.

"I say, whatever helps you
in your own life
is the right way,"
said Mrs. Santiago.

"I suppose you're right,"
said Gloria.
"And God knows
I need all the help I can get."

Thinking It Over

1. Have you ever gone on welfare?
   How did you feel about it?

2. How much do you take part
   in your neighborhood?

3. Do you have any interest
   in other religions?
   Why or why not?

6 Very Bad News

Of the three children
who went to school,
José Luis, the oldest,
"the good one,"
was doing the best.
He learned English fast.
He loved to read.
He seemed to do well
at everything he tried.

Carolina and José Miguel
were not doing as well.
They didn't want
to do their school work,
and José Miguel got into fights.
Gloria couldn't help with homework
because she couldn't speak English.
She worried
about what would happen
to these two children.

She also worried
about José Alonzo
back in Puerto Rico.
Hector wrote to say
that the boy
seemed well and happy
living with his *compadres.*
Still, Gloria wished
her other son
could be with her in New York.

She wished that Hector
would come back, too.
He wrote that his name
was still on the waiting list
at the radio factory.
He said he would get a job,
no matter what,
no matter where.
But he couldn't come
to New York
until he was sure
there was work for him.
He said he was a man,
and a man needed a job.

Then one night,
sitting out in front
of the apartment building,
Gloria heard some neighbors
talking about a new program.
The city fire department
would hire one minority person
for every three white people.
Puerto Ricans
were looked at as minorities.
The only catch
was that everyone
had to first pass
a Civil Service test in English.

Gloria got it into her mind
that maybe Hector
could become a firefighter.
Of course, he needed
to learn some English first.
Gloria hadn't seen her husband
with a book in his hands
since his school days
in Puerto Rico.
Would he go to school

to learn English
so he could get a job?

   Gloria couldn't wait
to talk with Hector
about this idea.
But everything turned upside down
the day she got the letter
from José Alonzo's *compadres*.
"We took good care
of your second son,"
Gloria read.
"What happened to him
was in God's hands,
not ours or Hector's.
There are too many cars
in San Juan.
One of those cars hit José Alonzo.
He was killed right away.
He went to his Lord above
without a fight.
He always loved you,
and we are sorry
that he was never able
to come be with you,
his dear mother."

The letter fell
from Gloria's hands.
Her head felt light
as she dropped
onto the chair
by her kitchen table.
She began to cry.

José Alonzo was dead.
The little boy
who always held his mother's hand
would never hold her hand again.
"I have five children left,"
Gloria said to herself.
"But there will always be six
in my heart.
I will always have love
for José Alonzo,
the one who is gone to heaven.
Oh, if only he had been with me!
Maybe he would still be with us."
She wished Hector were here now.

Gloria told Mrs. Santiago
the bad news.
"Would you like to talk

to your son one more time?"
Mrs. Santiago asked Gloria.

"What do you mean?
He is dead."

"There is a way,"
said Mrs. Santiago.

She took Gloria
down to the *botánica*.
They bought some herbs and incense
and walked over to the home
of a Puerto Rican woman
that Mrs. Santiago knew.
This woman, she said,
had special powers.
She knew how
to reach the world of the dead.

Gloria, Mrs. Santiago,
and the woman
sat around a table
and burned the incense.
The woman closed her eyes
and lifted her head

toward the sky.
"Do you hear me, José Alonzo?"
she said.
"Speak to me, José Alonzo.
Speak to me
and I will pass your words
along to your mother."

Gloria never heard
her dead son's voice.
But she felt him
in the room.
She told him
that God would take care of him.
She told him she loved him
and would never forget him.

After the visit
to the woman's apartment,
there was no question
in Gloria's mind
that José Alonzo was dead.
But as she flew to Puerto Rico
to go to his funeral,
she felt a little more at peace
about her loss.

Thinking It Over

1. What do you think
   makes some kids
   do well in school
   and others not do so well?

2. Have you or would you ever
   try to reach
   "the world of the dead"
   in such a way
   as Gloria did?
   Why or why not?

3. When someone you love dies,
   is there anything
   that helps you feel
   more at peace about it?

7 Together Is What Matters

Gloria and Hector
were glad to see each other
in Puerto Rico.
But the funeral for José Alonzo
was very, very sad
for both of them.

"I want you
to come along with me
back to New York,"
Gloria told Hector.
She told him
about the firefighter jobs.
She told him
about the English classes
held at the center
two blocks up
from their apartment.
She begged him
to fly back with her.

Sure enough,
Hector came along to New York.
But what really surprised Gloria
was that he started going
to English classes!
She knew how hard this must be
for a man like Hector.

"I never saw any need
to learn English,"
Hector said one night.
"I always got by without it.
But it's the only way
I can get a good job now.
I've made up my mind.
I'm going to go
for the firefighter test.
I'm going to make it."

Hector went to English class
four nights a week.
During the day
he worked in his English books.
He also found a part-time job
as a stock boy at the *bodega*.

A year later,
he felt ready
to take the Civil Service test.
And when he found out
that he had passed the test,
he almost couldn't believe it.
Next he had to get checked over
by a doctor
to make sure he was fit
to be a firefighter.
Then it was time
to start the training course.

At this point,
everything was looking up
for the Martinez family.
Then they heard the news
about their apartment building.

Hector read the letter
that came to them.
"Your building
will be torn down
to make way
for a new housing project.

You have 90 days
to find another place to live."

"We have lost our home!"
cried the little girls.

Gloria looked around
the tiny room
in which they sat.
A large rat ran toward the sink
looking for a bit of food.
"Another apartment
might be better than this rat ranch,"
Gloria said.
"Besides, this apartment
is not what makes a home.
A home is where the family is.
No matter where we live,
we have a home
if we are together."

"Your mother is right,"
said Hector.
Then he read
the rest of the letter.
"You may sign up

for public housing.
You must then wait your turn
to get an apartment.
It may be in any part
of the city."

   "What are we
going to do?"
Gloria asked.

   "We'll sign up
for public housing,"
said Hector.
"But while we wait,
we'll look for a place to live."

Thinking It Over

1. What would make you
   want to
   learn another language?

2. Why is it hard
   for some people
   to go back to school?

3. What are the first two things
   you would do
   if you found out
   that your building
   was going to be torn down?

8 To the South Bronx

The Martinez family
was very lucky.
They were able to get public housing
in the South Bronx.
They were glad
because the project
was in a part of New York
where other Puerto Ricans lived.

At first, Gloria
missed Spanish Harlem.
Most of all,
she missed Mrs. Santiago,
who had been a good friend
when she needed one.
Now it would be hard
to get to see her old neighbor.

The new apartment building
was 20 stories high.
All the buildings were very high.

The South Bronx
had *bodegas* and *botánicas,*
but Gloria had to walk a few blocks
to get to them.

   The worst thing
about the new place
was that José Miguel
started to hang out
with a gang of boys.
"What are we going to do
about that boy?"
Gloria asked Hector.
"He finds it so easy
to get into fights.
With this gang,
it will be much too easy."

   "We must keep him in at night,"
said Hector.
They tried to keep him at home,
but they couldn't watch him
every minute of the day.
Sometimes he didn't go to school.
Instead, he hung out with the gang.
Sometimes he left the apartment

in the middle of the night.
Hector and Gloria
did what they could,
but the boy seemed to find trouble
no matter what they did.

Then there was Carolina.
She was older now, too.
Many days she told her mother
she was too sick
to go to school.
Gloria tried to get the girl
to go to school,
but Carolina never went
more than three days a week.

Then one morning,
while Carolina was sleeping,
Gloria went into the room
where all the girls slept.
She began to look around.
She opened drawers
and looked inside them.
There, under a pile of clothes,
Gloria found
what she didn't want to find.

She knew it was a drug,
but she didn't know what kind.
She just took it out
and threw it in the trash
behind the building.

"What's become of these kids?"
said Hector.
"We try to raise them right.
How did they go so wrong?"

"We do try,"
said Gloria.
"But here in New York
it's too easy to find trouble.
Drugs and gangs are everywhere.
The kids can't get away
from all this stuff!"

"I can't have
such a wild daughter,"
said Hector.
"We'll send Carolina
back to Puerto Rico.
Our good friends there
will look after her

for a while.
I'm glad our little ones
are still all right.
And thank God for José Luis."

"The good one,"
said Gloria.

After school that day,
José Luis came home
with a big smile on his face.
"I want to join a club,"
he said very fast.

"It's not a gang, is it?"
Hector asked.

"No, no," said José Luis.
"It's a club at school.
It's called *Aspira*.
It's for kids like me
who would like to go to college."

"College?" said Gloria.
"No one in our family
has ever gone to college."

"Then I will be the first,"
said José Luis.
"*Aspira* tells Puerto Rican kids
to 'think college.'
They help us with English.
They help us
find money for college.
They help us get ready
in every way.
I want to join."

After all the trouble
with José Miguel and Carolina,
Hector and Gloria
couldn't say no to José Luis.
"You'll never make it
all the way to college,"
said Hector.

But Gloria was smiling.
"Come here, my good one,"
she said.
"You are too big now
to sit on my lap.
But I will give you a big kiss.
I know you will do fine."

Thinking It Over

1. If parents have
   a favorite child,
   what might this do
   to the other children
   in the family?

2. Has anyone in your family
   gone to college?
   How did they do it?

3. Would you like to go to college?
   What would you need to do
   before you could go?

9 Keeping Out of Trouble

Hector finished
the firefighter training course.
But then he had to wait
until a job opened up.
He began to spend some time
playing with the neighborhood kids
in the lot behind the project.
He could see that the kids
enjoyed playing baseball.
But they didn't really know
what they were doing.

"Put your hands like this,"
said Hector
as he showed one boy
how to hold a bat.
"Swing your bat
even with the ground,"
he told one girl.
More and more kids
began coming to Hector

for help with baseball.
Then he came up
with a great idea.
He set up teams
and filled the kids' time
with baseball games.
He could see that,
instead of doing drugs
and running with gangs,
these kids were playing sports.
Just about everyone
joined the sports program—
everyone except José Miguel,
Hector's own son.

"I can begin to understand
the problems of these kids,"
Gloria told Hector.
"They are young Puerto Ricans
who feel out of place.
They don't know who they are
here in New York.
They don't talk right.
They come from the wrong place.
They are poor.
You make them feel important."

"I wish I could do that
for our José Miguel,"
said Hector.

That same night,
a very bad thing happened.
A young woman
sitting in a school playground
was shot dead.
José Miguel came home
very upset.
"I had nothing to do with this,"
he cried.
"Believe me, I didn't."

"What happened?"
Gloria asked the boy.

"Some of the others in the gang
were shooting at some kid
who didn't pay them."

"You mean drug money?"
Gloria asked.

"Yes," said José Miguel.

"They hit the girl by mistake?"
asked Gloria.

"Yes," said José Miguel.
"But it wasn't me!"

"OK, OK," said Gloria.
"Now what are you
going to do about all this?"

"I want out of the gang,"
said José Miguel.

"Is it that easy?"
asked his mother.

"Maybe not,"
said José Miguel.
"But I would rather play baseball.
No one will hurt me
if I'm with my dad."

"You hope,"
said Gloria.
"Just stay out of trouble
and all my prayers are answered."

Thinking It Over

1. If you were out of work,
   what would be a good way
   to spend your time?

2. What can help
   to keep a kid
   out of trouble?

3. José feels safe
   when he is with his father.
   When do you feel safe?

10 Fighting Fires

At last, Hector got a job
as a city firefighter.
The news came in June,
right around Puerto Rican Day.
What a fine day for a party!

The whole family
went down to Manhattan.
The Puerto Rican Day parade
marched up Fifth Avenue.
Young people sang and danced
and threw flowers
into the crowd.
All the Puerto Rican clubs
had bright-colored floats
about their towns in Puerto Rico.
The sounds of *bongos* and *congas*
filled the air.
It was a great day.

Then Hector's job began.
It was a very hard time.
The old apartment buildings
in the South Bronx
were catching on fire
one after another.
It was Hector's job
to fight those fires.
He kept up
the sports program, too.

"I worry about you,"
said Gloria one night.
"Your job is not safe."

"Fire-fighting
is not always safe work,"
said Hector.
"But we are as careful
as we can be.
I don't worry about myself.
I worry about all these people
who must leave their homes.
Most of them have no place to go.
They are just out on the street.
It's very sad."

Just then, Hector was called out
for yet another fire.
He grabbed
one last bite of rice and beans
and headed for the firehouse.

This was a very big fire.
Some people were killed.
It took all night
to bring the fire under control.
Hector began to head for home.
Then he heard a child's voice.
It was a tiny cry,
coming from inside the building.
Hector followed the sound.
He looked and looked,
and then he spotted
a small girl,
sitting in a corner
under a table.
"I can't find my mother,"
she cried.

Hector picked her up
and carried her home.
"You can stay with us

until we find your mother,"
Gloria told the child.
"We can make room
for one more."

Hector and Gloria
told the police
that they were taking care
of the girl.
Days, weeks, and months passed.
The little girl's mother
was never found.
She must have died
in the fire.
So Hector and Gloria
became the girl's
foster parents.
"We are her *compadres*,"
said Gloria.
"We will raise her
like one of our own."

Gloria felt the hole in her heart
that was left when José Alonzo died.
It didn't feel so empty now.

Thinking It Over

1. Have you ever gone to
   or been part of
   a Puerto Rican Day parade?
   How about another
   kind of parade?
   What was it like?

2. Would you like a job
   that was not always safe?

3. Could your family
   ever take in a child
   who needed a home?

4. Have you ever felt
   "a hole in your heart"?
   Did you ever find a way
   to fill that hole?

11 New Plans

The next few years
were filled with good times and bad.
Carolina stayed in Puerto Rico.
Then José Miguel
dropped out of school
and went to Puerto Rico, too.
Hector kept on fighting fires.
And José Luis
not only went to college
but also went on to law school.

"I am happy for our children,"
said Gloria to Hector.
"Carolina and José Miguel
are doing OK in Puerto Rico.
José Luis will be a lawyer.
The younger ones are in school
here in New York.
All of this is very good.
But will we ever again
be all together in one place?"

"Being together would be good,"
said Hector.
"But it is not something
we should hope for.
We decided years ago
to come to New York.
We knew it would be easy
to go back to Puerto Rico
and back here again.
Nothing else about our life
has been easy, however!
We do the best we can.
But having our family
all in one place—
maybe this is too much to ask."

"I suppose you are right,"
said Gloria.
"Maybe being together
is not God's will."

Then, during José Luis's
third and last year in law school,
he was sent to Camden, New Jersey.
He had the job of working
with low-income Puerto Ricans there.

Camden was a city
in the southern part of New Jersey,
near Philadelphia, Pennsylvania.
Many Puerto Ricans
had moved there from New York.
José Luis had lots of work to do
for the people in Camden.
He got to know about
many programs going on in Camden.
One housing program
really got his interest.

The next time
he visited his family in New York,
he told them about the program.
"We can buy a house for only $100!"
he told everyone.

"Only $100 to buy a house?"
Hector asked.

"The houses are in bad shape,"
José Luis explained.
"The house we get
will need a lot of work.
But the city will help us

pay to fix it up.
Then, if we do all the work
and live in the house
for three years,
it will be our very own home!
Look at us!
We can all work together!
I think we should do it!"

"But where do we live
until the house is ready?"
Gloria wanted to know.

José Luis had everything planned.
"We'll go to Camden on weekends
while the weather is warm,"
he said.
"We can fix up the place
just enough to sleep in it.
Then when winter comes,
we can live in the house
while we paint it
and finish up everything."

"What about my job?"
said Hector.

"I waited a long time
for a job in the fire department.
And I've been there
for a good many years now."

"They need firefighters
down in Camden, too,"
said José Luis.
"You'll get a job."

"I don't know
if we want to leave New York,"
said Gloria.

"Camden is not heaven,"
said José Luis.
"But New York isn't, either.
If you don't like Camden,
you can always move back
to New York.
What do you say?"

"I say, let's do it,"
said Hector.
"Let's buy a house for $100
and make it into a home."

Thinking It Over

1. What are some programs
   in your area
   that can help people?
   Which programs
   are of most interest
   to you and your family?

2. If you could buy a house
   for just $100
   and then fix it up,
   would you do it?

3. Would you ever move
   to a different place
   if you could have
   a better life there?
   Why or why not?

12 A Home in Camden

The city of Camden
found a house
for the Martinez family.
No question about it,
the place was in bad shape.
The walls were falling down.
The water pipes didn't work.
The heat didn't work, either.
All the windows
were boarded up.
Bricks were falling out
onto the street.

"We have our work
cut out for us,"
said Hector
as he looked the place over.
"It's also a real fire trap."
Firefighter that he was,
the first thing Hector did
was put in a smoke alarm.

The Martinez family
followed José Luis's plan.
On week-ends,
they went down to Camden.
A man
from the housing department
helped them get started.
He explained
what they would have to do.

Then they got busy.
They built new walls.
They covered them with drywall.
They hammered.
They sanded.
They put in new pipes.
They got the heat working.
They put on a new roof.
They did everything
the house needed to have done.
By the time winter came,
the place was warm and dry.

Late that fall,
word came from Puerto Rico.
Carolina and José Miguel

had heard about
what their family was doing.
They both decided to come north
and help out.
The brother and sister
flew up together.
They found their way
to Camden, New Jersey.
They found the house
where the rest of their family
was now living.

Gloria cried
when she saw her son and daughter.
"I have not seen you
for so many years!"
she said.
"I love you so much!"
She held them both in her arms.
She couldn't make herself let go.

That night,
Gloria made a big dinner.
There was no table,
so the men put a big board
across two sawhorses.

Gloria threw a sheet
over the board
and put out her best dishes.
Then Hector raised a glass
to make a toast.

"Let me make the toast,"
said Gloria.
"To our family,
together in one place.
Bless us and our home!"

She looked at each face
around the board table.
There was Hector,
her dear husband.
There was José Luis,
the oldest child.
There were Carolina
and José Miguel,
fresh from Puerto Rico.
There were the twins,
Inez and Susana.
And there was the little girl
who had come to them
out of the apartment building fire.

Gloria couldn't believe
they were all here,
at one table.
She prayed for José Alonzo.
Then she prayed
that she would remember this day
for the rest of her life.

The next morning,
José Luis was hard at work
by the time
Carolina and José Miguel
came down for breakfast.
As soon as they finished eating,
they started to walk
upstairs again.

"Where are you going?"
José Luis asked them.
"There's work to be done!
Come back here!
If we move fast enough,
we'll have the living room
finished by tonight!"

With that,
he handed Carolina a paintbrush
and José Miguel a hammer.

Gloria watched all this
and smiled to herself.
"Ah, the good one,"
she said out loud.
"I always called José Luis
'the good one.'
But you are all good ones.
Every one of you.
I love you all."

And sure enough,
by the time it got dark that night,
the living room was finished.

Thinking It Over

1. Has there ever been something that your whole family worked on together?

2. What makes family members want to be together?

3. What *keeps* families together?